New in Town

by KEVIN CORNELL

FARRAR STRAUS GIROUX
NEW YORK

FOR KIM, WHO HOLDS MY HAND.

AND GRACE, FOR HER WISDOM, WIT, and SUPPORT.

Farrar Straus Giroux Books for Young Readers
An imprint of Macmillan Publishing Group, LLC
120 Broadway, New York, NY 10271

COLOR SEPARATIONS BY: Bright Arts (H.K.) Ltd.
PRINTED IN: China by Toppan Leefung Printing Ltd.,
Dongguan City, Guangdong Province

Edited by Grace Kendall
Designed by Sharismar Rodriguez

FIRST EDITION 2021

1 3 5 7 9 10 8 6 4 2

mackids.com

LIBRARY of CONGRESS CONTROL NUMBER: 2020011064
ISBN: 978-0-374-30609-0

OUR BOOKS MAY BE PURCHASED
IN BULK FOR PROMOTIONAL, EDUCATIONAL,
OR BUSINESS USE. PLEASE CONTACT YOUR LOCAL
BOOKSELLER OR THE MACMILLAN CORPORATE
and PREMIUM SALES DEPARTMENT at
(800) 221-7945 EXT. 5442 OR BY EMAIL at
macmillanspecialmarkets@macmillan.com.

One fine morning, the people of Puddletrunk woke to find...

...their bridge had collapsed.

Again.

Over the years, they'd lost many a bridge.

bridge 181

74

PUDDLE
TRUNK
←

#63

WELCOME TO PUDDLETRUNK

Termites, sad to say, had destroyed them all.

CHOMPING BITS

WALKING BITS

FLYING BITS

CHOMPING BITS

THE DREADFUL TERMITE!!

BITE RADIUS

informative guide provided by the fabulous M. Gulch

New Bridge Erected

THANKS TO LOCAL BRIDGE TROLL

THE HOT, DRY SOUTH — A recent arrival to our fair little burgh, a Mr. Mortimer Gulch of Gulch Gulch, has generously offered to

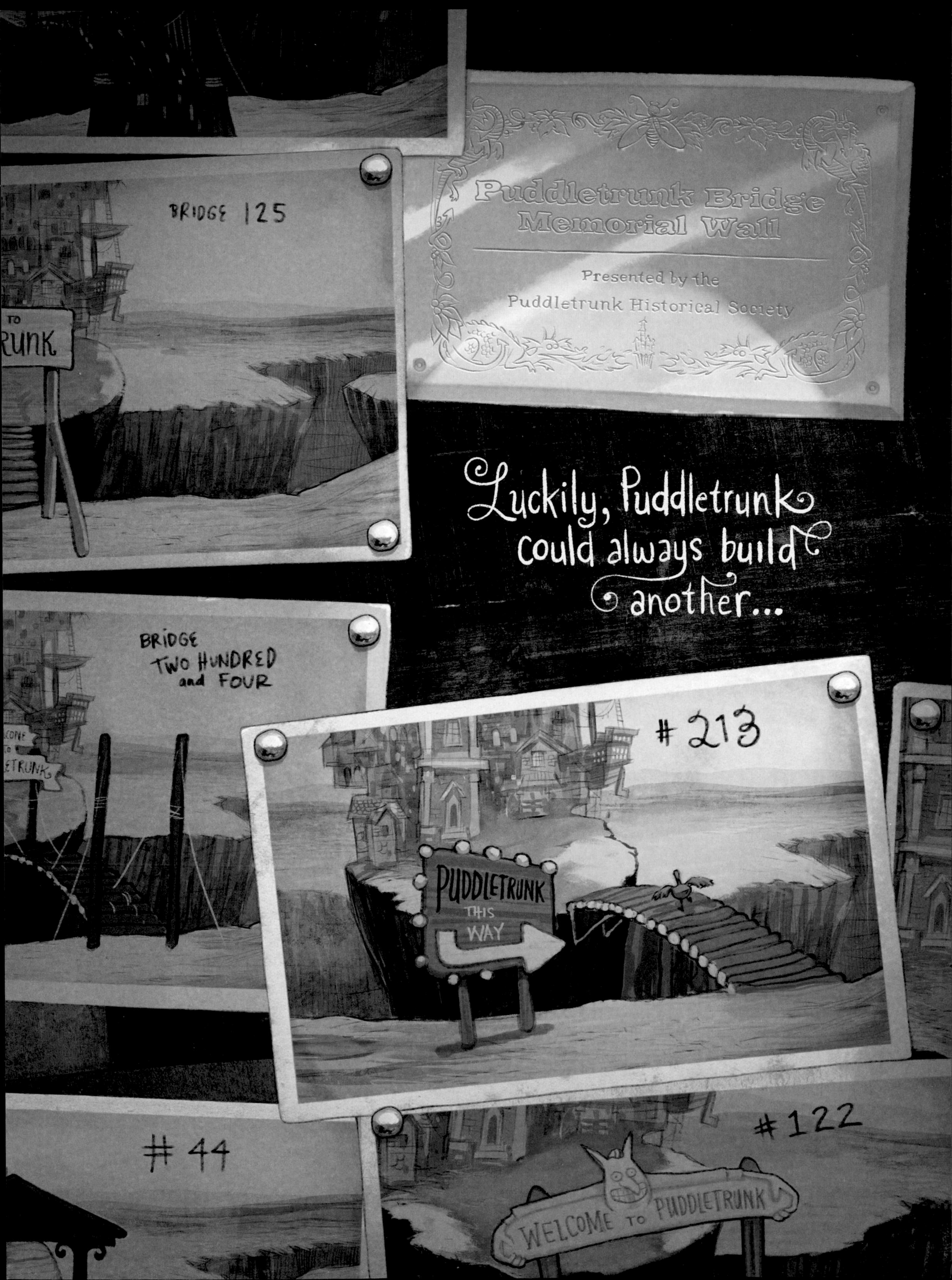

BRIDGE 125
TO
RUNK
Puddletrunk Bridge Memorial Wall
Presented by the
Puddletrunk Historical Society
BRIDGE TWO HUNDRED and FOUR
213
PUDDLETRUNK
THIS WAY
44
122
WELCOME TO PUDDLETRUNK

Luckily, Puddletrunk could always build another...

"Come now, little fellow," urged Mr. Gulch. "Everyone else donates!"

"Then my donation," replied the repairman, "will be to fix your clock tower free of charge."

... a MASTER of
MOTIVATIONAL
RHETORIC...

And the bridge was quite good, too.

Until, that is, the wood ran out.

Mr. Gulch
thought this
reply quite
ignorant.

Towers, in fact, were
just as delicious as bridges!
Perhaps even more so!

Luckily, he was there to speak words of comfort to the angry townsfolk, as they stumbled from their slumber.

And, my stars, it was true! The fallen tower now spanned both sides of the chasm and made for a magnificent bridge!

So overjoyed were
the folk of Puddletrunk...

...that they
threw the grandest of
grand openings!

Everyone enjoyed themselves immensely!

As for the repairman, well... there was still plenty in Puddletrunk, that needed fixing — so he decided to stay!

And though he was new in town, and did not know how things worked...

...as far as
the folk of
Puddletrunk
were concerned...

273
WELCOME TO
PUDDLETRUNK

SOLD

...that was something
TRULY fabulous.

BRIDGE
#273